HELLO! WELCOME TO THE FABUMOUSE WORLD OF THE THEA SISTERS!

D0289327

Thea Sisters

Hi, I'm Thea Stilton, Geronimo Stilton's sister! I am a special reporter for <u>The Rodent's Gazette</u>, the most famous newspaper on Mouse Island. I love traveling and meeting new mice all over the world, like the Thea Sisters. These five friends have helped me out with my adventures. Let me introduce you to these fabumouse young mice!

Colette has a real passion for fashion. She loves to design her own clothes in her favorite color, pink.

Violet loves studying and learning new things. She is a fan of classical music and dreams of becoming a famouse violinist someday.

Pamela loves pizza so much she eats it for breakfast. She is a skilled mechanic who can fix just about any motor she gets her paws on.

PAULINA is shy and loves to read about faraway places. But she loves traveling to those places even more.

Nicky is from the Australian Outback, where she developed a love of nature and the environment. This outdoors-loving mouse is always on the move.

Thea Sisters

Thea Stilton

MOUSEFORD ACADEMY

THE SECRET NOTEBOOK

Scholastic Inc.

Copyright © 2011 by Edizioni Piemme S.p.A., Palazzo Mondadori, Via Mondadori 1, 20090 Segrate, Italy. International Rights © Atlantyca S.p.A. English translation © 2017 by Atlantyca S.p.A.

The publisher does not have any control over and does not assume any responsibility for author or third-party websites or their content.

GERONIMO STILTON and THEA STILTON names, characters, and related indicia are copyright, trademark, and exclusive license of Atlantyca S.p.A. All rights reserved. The moral right of the author has been asserted. Based on an original idea by Elisabetta Dami.

www.geronimostilton.com

Published by Scholastic Inc., *Publishers since 1920*, 557 Broadway, New York, NY 10012. SCHOLASTIC and associated logos are trademarks and/or registered trademarks of Scholastic Inc.

Stilton is the name of a famous English cheese. It is a registered trademark of the Stilton Cheese Makers' Association. For more information, go to www.stiltoncheese.com.

No part of this publication may be reproduced, stored in a retrieval system, or transmitted in any form or by any means, electronic, mechanical, photocopying, recording, or otherwise, without written permission of the copyright holder. For information regarding permission, please contact: Atlantyca S.p.A., Via Leopardi 8, 20123 Milan, Italy; e-mail foreignrights@atlantyca.it, www.atlantyca.com.

This book is a work of fiction. Names, characters, places, and incidents are either the product of the author's imagination or are used fictitiously, and any resemblance to actual persons, living or dead, business establishments, events, or locales is entirely coincidental.

ISBN 978-1-338-11659-5

Text by Thea Stilton
Original title *Il club delle poetesse*
Cover by Giuseppe Facciotto
Illustrations by Chiara Balleello (pencils), and Francesco Castelli (color)
Graphics by Yuko Egusa

Special thanks to Tracey West
Translated by Anna Pizzelli
Interior design by Becky James

10 9 8 7 6 5 4 3 2   17 18 19 20 21

Printed in the U.S.A.   40
First printing 2017

A CLUE IN VERSE

It was a beautiful day at Mouseford Academy. But instead of enjoying the sunshine, Violet was stuck indoors feeling sorry for herself.

"Achoo!" She sneezed.

Poor Violet was recovering from the flu. She had been in bed for several days, and although she was feeling better, she was tired of being sick.

Her roommates, Nicky and Paulina, were staying in Colette and Pam's room until Violet got better.

"Ugh, I'm so bored!" Violet exclaimed with a loud sigh.

Even though her FEVER was gone, her friends had insisted that she stay in BED one more day. Violet knew they were right, but she was itching to get back to the whirlwind of lessons and ACTIVITIES at Mouseford Academy.

In the meantime, she tried to come up with anti-boredom remedies. First, she made a list of every CHEESE she'd ever eaten. Then she organized her books alphabetically. She tried to read the **fashion magazines** that Colette had brought her, but they weren't very interesting.

Then Violet started doodling on the magazine covers with a marker, which turned out to be fun. She was busy turning a **supermodel** into a **CLOWN** when there was a knock on her door.

"Come in!" Violet called out, and *Colette*, *Nicky*, *Pamela*, and PAULINA stepped inside. Together, the five friends called themselves the **THEA SISTERS**.

"Finally, you're here!" she squeaked. "What's the **news**? How was the first English class? What **B O O K S** is Professor Rattcliff having us read this semester?"

"Hey, **SLOW DOWN**, Violet," Pam said. "One question at a time!"

Violet took a deep breath. "Sorry. I'm just so **excited**! You've got to tell me about

English class. You know it's my favorite."

Paulina smiled. "Well, we're not reading any NOVELS," she said.

"We're not?" Violet asked, puzzled.

Nicky shook her head. "Nope. And no *short stories*, either."

"And no **PLAYS**," Colette added.

"Then what will we be reading?" Violet asked, curious.

"Since you're my friend, I'll give you a CLUE," Pam replied. "We'll read some that don't rhyme and others that DO."

Violet grinned. "I get it now. We're going to study poetry!"

"Exactly!" Pam exclaimed, clapping her paws.

"How exciting," Violet replied, her eyes shining. "I **love** poetry!"

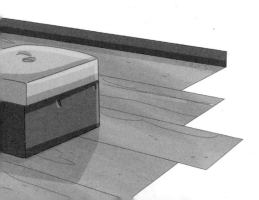

POETRY FEVER!

Violet returned to her classes the next day. During Professor Margaret Rattcliff's class, she could barely contain her excitement as she read the list of all the poets they were going to study.

"My **FEVER** may be gone," she said to Colette when class was over, "but I think I have another fever."

"Oh no, really?" Colette asked.

Violet grinned. "Yes. Poetry fever!"

And Violet wasn't the only student who had been infected by the poetry bug. After a week of class, just about everyone was discussing their favorite poems and *poets.*

In fact, Violet and her friends got into a

HEATED DISCUSSION about their favorite poets one afternoon in the cafeteria.

Pam spotted Professor Rattcliff and called her over. "Can you please give us your opinion?" Pam asked.

"Of course," the professor replied.

"These mouselets are certain that Elizabeth Barrett Browning is the best poet," Ryder said.

You're wrong!

"But they're **WRONG!**" added his friend Ron.

That's your opinion!

"No, you're wrong! She **IS** the best poet!" Elly insisted enthusiastically.

"She writes about things that matter, like **love** and **life**."

Colette nodded in agreement. "Elizabeth

Barrett Browning's words are so beautiful!" she said, and then she began to recite one of her favorite poems:

"How do I love thee?
Let me count the ways.
I love thee to the depth
and breadth and height
My soul can reach,
when feeling out of sight . . . "

Nicky sighed. "Wow, that is beautiful."

"It's nice, but poems can make you feel **powerful**, too," Ron argued. "Like the poems of Walt Whitman."

"Yes!" Craig agreed enthusiastically. He jumped up on a chair and recited:

"O Captain! my Captain!
our fearful trip is done,

The ship has weather'd every rack, the prize we sought is won."

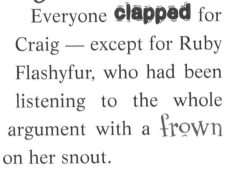

O Captain!

Everyone **clapped** for Craig — except for Ruby Flashyfur, who had been listening to the whole argument with a frown on her snout.

"I just don't get it," she said. "It's all pretty boring to me."

Professor Rattcliff cleared her throat. "I am happy to see that poetry is spurring such **interesting** discussions," she said with a smile. "However, this isn't an argument that I can settle. Any poet who touches your soul is a good poet. Now, if you'll excuse me, my **TEA** is getting cold."

As the professor walked away, Tanja leaned in and whispered to her friends. "I have an idea," she said **MYSTERIOUSLY**. "Let's meet in the garden after class!"

Elizabeth Barrett Browning (1806–1861)

She was one of the most famous Victorian poets and was popular in England and the United States.

Walt Whitman (1819–1892)

An American poet and journalist, his best known work is the poetry collection *Leaves of Grass*.

A POETRY CLUB!

"I wonder where she is," Pam mused.

The **Last class** of the day was over, and a group of mouselets was waiting in the garden for Tanja: the Thea Sisters; Ruby and her friends, the Ruby Crew; and Tanja's best friend, Elly.

"I have **BETTER THINGS** to do than sit around here," Ruby complained impatiently.

"There she is!" Elly cried as Tanja ran toward them with a **Bulky** bag slung over her shoulder.

"Sorry I'm **late**," Tanja apologized, catching her breath.

"What's in the bag?" Ruby asked.

Tanja grinned. "I stopped at the ThRiFTy

R**at** and got us these!" She gave a **colorful notebook** to each of her friends.

"Thanks," Nicky said. "But what are they for?"

"To *write* our poetry!" Tanja announced.

"You mean, write our **own** poems?" Violet asked a little nervously.

"Exactly," Tanja replied. "I think we should form a **poetry club**!"

"What, exactly, is a poetry club?" Pam wanted to know.

"We can write our own poems and have **poetry readings**," she said, her blue eyes shining with excitement. "And we can meet in the **LIZARD LOUNGE**!"

Paulina clapped her paws together. "**I LOVE THAT IDEA!**"

"We'll need to decorate the Lizard Lounge to fit the theme," Elly suggested.

"We can add comfortable, **COLORFUL** pillows," Paulina said.

"I love it!" Colette said. "And we could wear more poetic **clothes** and give ourselves poetic **nicknames**. I'd like to be . . . *Lady Colette*!"

"And we could eat poetic **snacks**," Pam added. "Like tiny cheese sandwiches with the crusts cut off."

"**Fabumouse**!" Nicky exclaimed. "This will be fun."

> **POETRY CLUB:**
> **To-Do List**
> ✹ Decorate the clubhouse.
> ✹ Pick poetic nicknames.
> ✹ Wear inspiring clothing.
> ✹ Get poetic snacks.

"Maybe you think it's fabumouse, but I don't!" Ruby said, annoyed.

"Why not?" Tanja asked.

"Because poetry makes me **yawn**!" Ruby snapped. She turned to the Ruby Crew. "Let's go. We don't want to be in this **boring** club."

She **TOSSED** her notebook on the ground and walked away, followed by her friends.

"If there were a club for **rude** mouselets, Ruby would definitely be its president!" Pam exclaimed.

Her friends shook their heads, laughing.

Humpf!

"That's Ruby for you," Paulina said. "But that's okay. We can still have a **poetry club** without her!"

A SECRET MEETING

The members of the brand-new poetry club got busy right away. First, they decorated the Lizard Lounge with big pillows for the floor. They brought in flowers and electric candles to set the mood.

That night, they got to work writing their poems. By the next afternoon, they were all ready for the FIRST meeting. Each club member brought in an object to represent the poem she had created.

"It looks beautiful in here," Tanja remarked, looking around. "A perfect setting for poetry readings!"

The other mouselets all agreed that the room was perfect.

"So, should we start reading our poems?" Pam asked.

"Not yet," Colette replied. "I think we should all reveal the nicknames we've chosen."

"Good idea," Paulina agreed. "I'll go first. I'm inspired by beautiful COLORS. So I'm choosing the nickname Rainbow."

"Love it!" Nicky said. "And I'm writing poems about NATURE, so I'm going with the nickname River."

"I would like to be called Melody," Violet chimed in. "Because I've been listening to music to inspire my writing."

"I've been writing poetry when I look at the sea," Elly said. "So I'd like to be called Sea Star."

"That's a good one for you, Elly," Tanja said. "I'd like to be LILIJA, after my

Poetry club

Lady Colette

INSPIRATIONAL OBJECT: A heart headband, to represent romantic poems.

Rainbow

INSPIRATIONAL OBJECT: A ribbon with the colors Paulina loves.

River

INSPIRATIONAL OBJECT: A Green Mice pin from Nicky's favorite nature organization.

Liliya

INSPIRATIONAL OBJECT: A Russian nesting doll ring from Tanja's homeland.

Sea Star

INSPIRATIONAL OBJECT: A shell bracelet, to represent the ocean.

Melody

INSPIRATIONAL OBJECT: A clef symbol necklace, because music inspires Violet.

Brooklyn

INSPIRATIONAL OBJECT: A baseball cap from Pam's favorite pizza place.

grandmother back in Russia. She read me poems when I was just a little **mouseling**."

"What about you, Pam?" Nicky asked. "Will you be **Pepperoni**, because you love **PIZZA** so much?"

"Ha, very funny!" Pam replied. "But no.

Let's rap!

Where I come from, **rap music** is the best poetry. So you can call me **Brooklyn**!"

Tanja stood up. "Now that we've introduced ourselves," she began, "I, Liliya, declare the first meeting of the **poetry club** officially open!"

"I'll go first," Paulina offered. She sat in the big **red chair** that the mouselets had designated as their Poem Throne.

Meanwhile, down the hall in the Gecko Lounge, Ryder was talking to the other Gecko Club members.

"I think the Lizard Club is hiding something," he said.

"I do, too!" Shen agreed, adjusting his glasses as he spoke. "Did you notice how they were **whispering** to each other at lunch today?"

Grunt!

Craig was working on his **biceps**, using a dictionary as a dumbbell. "What do you think they're up to?"

"I'm not sure," Ron replied, "but I think I know where they are. I saw Tanja RUSHING into the Lizard Lounge just a few minutes ago."

The four young rodents **LOOKED** at one another.

"Let's go **FIND OUT** what they're up to!" Craig cried.

RHYME TIME

"Orange makes my heart feel warm.
Gray is like a coming storm.
Purple makes me rock and roll.
Colors sparkle in my soul!"

Paulina's friends **clapped** as she finished her poem.

"**Well done**!" Colette cheered.

The other members of the poetry club took their turns. Tanja (Liliya) read a poem about a **SLED RACE**. Then Lady Colette read a poem titled "Love at First Sight," dedicated to . . . a **PURSE**!

After that, Pam (Brooklyn) started rapping about gorgonzola **PIZZA**!

The pizza poem made everyone **hungry**,

so they broke for a snack.
Then Elly (Sea Star) read
a poem about a **coral**

reef. Nicky (River) followed
with a beautiful poem about the sound of
the wind blowing through tree branches.

"Your turn, Melody," Nicky said to Violet
as she got off the Poem Throne.

Violet looked down at her paws. "I, um, I
didn't write anything yet," she said. "I just
wasn't feeling any inspiration."

Actually, Violet was afraid to tell her
friends the truth: she was too **shy** to read
her poem out loud!

"Next time, then," Pam said, and then . . .

The loud noise came from just outside
their door.

Tanja opened the door and found Ron, Craig, Ryder, and Shen standing there!

"What are you doing here?" Tanja asked suspiciously.

"Um, we were just looking at this PAINTING," Ryder said innocently.

"We love art, don't we, Geckos?"

The other members of the poetry club stepped into the hall. "If you ask me, it looks like you were **SPYING** on us," Pam accused.

Craig held up his paws. "All right, we confess! We were cuⓇious about what you were up to."

"And now that we know you have a poetry club, we think it's a great idea," Ron added. "In fact, if you don't mind, we'd like to form our own."

"I don't see why not," Tanja said. "Mouseford Academy could use more poets!"

WORK IN PROGRESS

The Gecko Club called their group the Rhyming Rats. They began having meetings, too. Soon, the Academy was buzzing about the two clubs. Professor Rattcliff was very **proud** of her students, and that made one mouselet very JEALOUS.

"Did you see how **PLeaSeD** Professor Rattcliff is with the Thea Sisters?" Ruby **complained** to the Ruby Crew after class.

"Yes, but Tanja did ask us to join the club," Zoe pointed out.

"Clubs are supposed to be fun," Ruby shot back. "It's bad enough we have to do poetry in class!"

"I don't love poetry, either, but I do like

the way they decorated the Lizard
Lounge," Alicia said.

Ruby's GREEN eyes widened. Alicia
had given her an **idea**!

"I know what to do!" Ruby cried, and then
she RUSHED off to her room, leaving her
puzzled friends behind.

Ruby hated to see other students getting
more attention than she was. She called
her mom on her cell phone.

"Hi, Mom, it's Ruby," she said. "I was just wondering if you could help out with a little PROJECT here. The school's Lizard Lounge really needs a big reNOVatioN. Could you send your decorator out here right away?"

Rebecca Flashyfur neveR said no to her daughter. Ruby ended the call and grinned. The poetry club wouldn't be able to meet if they didn't have a CLUBHOUSE!

The next day, the Thea Sisters followed a trail of PAINT CANS and brushes down the hall leading to the Lizard Lounge. When they got to the door, a rodent in work clothes held up his paw.

"Sorry, you can't come in," he said.

"Since when?" Nicky asked. "And who are you?"

"I'm in charge of the renovation," he replied. Then he explained that the Lizard

Lounge was going to be under **construction** for a while.

The Thea Sisters *RACED* to the headmaster's office. When they arrived, they found him talking to *Ruby* and a stylish-looking mouse — her mom's interior *decorator*.

"Hello, students!" Headmaster de Mousus greeted them. "I have **GOOD news**! Thanks to Ruby and the kindness of the Flashyfur family, you will have a *brand-new* Lizard Lounge in a month or so."

"What a **coincidence**," Pam mumbled. But the headmaster looked so **happy** that the Thea Sisters didn't want to complain. They left without voicing their *suspicions* about Ruby's motive.

AN UNEXPECTED FIND

"Are you thinking what I'm thinking?" Paulina asked her friends in the hallway.

"Yes," Colette replied. "With this renovation, Ruby is trying to **END** the poetry club!"

"Right, but we have no PROOF," Nicky pointed out.

Professor Rattcliff walked up as they were talking. "Do you know what's going on in the Lizard Lounge?" she asked. "Someone's making a big commotion there. It woke me up early!"

"We woke up to a very unpleasant **SURPRISE**, too," Pam said. Then she told the professor about the renovation.

"Now the poetry club has no clubhouse," Violet concluded **sadly**.

The professor smiled. "Well, **earplugs** will solve my problem. And I think I have a **solution** for yours. Follow me!"

Professor Rattcliff led them to a small room near the library.

"You could turn this room into your new **CLUBHOUSE**," she said, opening the door. "It's where we store **B O O K S** that we've taken off the library shelves."

The poetry club members looked around the room. It was **dusty** and COBWEBS hung from the ceiling. **Shaky** piles of books rose up from the floor.

"Well, it definitely has a **literary** atmosphere," Elly said.

"But what about . . . achoo . . . the dust?" Colette asked.

"A little dust can't stop us!" Pam cried.

"This place just needs a good **cleaning**," Tanja said. "Let's get to work!"

The mouselets quickly got busy. Elly and Violet **dusted** and got rid of the

SPIDERWEBS. Tanja, Colette, and Paulina managed to get the COLORFUL cushions back from the Lizard Lounge. Pam and Nicky came up with a creative way to use the piles of books as FURNITURE.

"All done!" Nicky exclaimed, admiring the room's new coffee table.

Then she held up a small book bound in **red leather**. "We found this in one of the piles. It looks like a diary!"

Violet took it from her and flipped through the pages. "You're right! It was written forty years ago by someone with the initials M.R.!"

"Ooh, how **mysterious**!" Colette said.

All of the mouselets gathered around

Violet, eager to see the diary. The YELLOWED pages smelled of forgotten SECRETS. Violet cleared her throat and began to read out loud.

Dear Diary . . .

OUR ADVENTURE BEGINS . . .

Dear Diary,

What a day! Just think — only yesterday, I was still at Mouseford Academy, trying to close my stuffed suitcase. Today, I'm in Rome, Italy! How fabumouse!

We had a nice flight, but things got tricky when we got to the hotel. Charlotte, Deb, Pilar, Sunny, and I had booked two rooms to share, but only one was available! We were told that another student had demanded the room so that she and her friends could have a whole floor to themselves.

Who would do such a thing and get away with it? Well, it turns out that Priscilla Poshpaws was the student, and her father owns the hotel! You should have seen how much luggage she had with her. (Even more than Charlotte, and she never travels with less than six bags!)

CHARLOTTE'S MOUNTAIN OF SUITCASES!

So the five of us had to squeeze into one room. Luckily, Deb insisted that the concierge find us at least two extra cots. There is hardly any room to move around now, and our luggage is piled up everywhere, but the fun is doubled!

That's all for now, diary. Tomorrow is the first day of summer session, and I want to look good!

M. R.

P.S. A new adventure is about to begin! ☺

PAGE AFTER
PAGE . . .

Violet closed the diary.

"Hey!" Pam squeaked. "We don't know what this summer session is all about. Why did you **STOP**?"

"Because we have DANCE class with Professor Plié in five minutes!" Tanja cried, **JUMPING** up.

"**Holey cheese**! You're right!" Pam exclaimed, slapping her forehead. "This diary is so intriguing that we lost track of time!"

We're late!

The mouselets DASHED to the dance studio, but their THOUGHTS were still in that new clubhouse. Who was the **mysterious** writer, M.R.? And what were a group of Mouseford students doing in Rome for the summer?

Before they entered dance class, Colette stopped her friends. "Let's get back to the **CLUBHOUSE** this afternoon," she suggested. "I am so curious to find out more about this diary writer and her Roman holiday. We can read more of the diary during our poetry club meeting!"

The others agreed that this was a good idea. They all met up again that afternoon, and over the next few days, they spent every **FREE** moment reading the diary.

It was impossible not to get sucked into the story! The mouselets found out that the mysterious writer and her friends had traveled to **Rome** from Mouseford

to attend a summer school for talented *writers*. During that summer, each group of students had to create a magazine. The best one would win a PRIZE from an international jury of judges.

UNEXPECTED HELP!

Dear Diary,

Never judge a book by its cover, and never judge a day by the morning! Charlotte, Sunny, Pilar, Deb, and I spent the morning on the balcony, trying to come up with an idea for our magazine. But no luck!

We had plenty of ideas. Charlotte suggested a fashion magazine. Deb thought we could do an illustrated magazine that showed how to fix cars. They are good ideas, but we needed something really special to stand out.

ELENA AND TERESA: OUR ROMAN FRIENDS!

We were about to give up when something unexpected happened! Elena and Teresa came onto the balcony. They both go to the Academy di Mouzza in Rome and are part of the summer session. We started chatting (Pilar asked for directions to the library, and Sunny wanted to know where the parks were), when the magazine came up.

It turns out that Elena and Teresa were stuck on an idea, too, so we decided to join forces! We still don't know what the magazine will be about, but we do know that it will be special, because it will be the result of teamwork!

Tomorrow we're having our first meeting! Can't wait!

M. R. ☺

An Invisible Clue!

"It's incredible!" Colette exclaimed. "The longer we read the diary, the more I feel I have known these five mouselets forever . . ."

Her friends sighed. Each one of them could recognize themselves in the Mouseford students from forty years ago. And more than that, they knew that the mouselets in the diary shared a STRONG BOND of friendship — just like they did!

The diary turned out to be full of SURPRISES. Each time they read it, they learned something new. That afternoon . . .

"Hold on a second, Violet," Tanja said. "Could you read the last sentence again?"

Violet repeated the sentence she had just read. "I was thinking about the time capsule we **buried** last summer at Mouseford."

"What's a time capsule?" Tanja asked, puzzled.

"You don't know?" Nicky asked. "You put objects important to you in a BOX, and then you seal it and hide it. Then when it's opened years later, it's like a WINDOW into the past."

It holds your most important memories!

Everyone had the same **thought** at once. If M.R. and her friends had created a time capsule forty years ago, then it might still be **hidden** somewhere in Mouseford!

"**We have to find it!**" Elly exclaimed, excited.

"Yes, but how? The diary doesn't say where the time capsule is hidden," Violet said, flipping through the pages. "But I do see something unusual: a BLANK page, right in the middle of the book."

Paulina's ears PERKED UP. "A blank page? Let me see."

Sniff!

She took the book from Violet — and sniffed it!

The others watched her curiously.

"Aha!" she cried, grinning. "Just like I thought. LEMON! I think I've found a clue."

Her friends looked at her, puzzled.

"It's an old form of SECRET WRITING," Paulina explained.

"You could write a secret message in **invisible ink**, and the receiver of the message would know what to do to make it visible. In this case, the invisible ink is just simple LEMON JUICE!"

"How does it work?" Colette asked.

"You dip a **paintbrush** in lemon juice and then you write your message with the brush, like you would with a pen," Paulina explained.

"And then how do you read the message?" Nicky asked.

"All you need is some **HEAT**," Paulina replied. "It makes the writing appear."

"What are we waiting for?" Pam asked. "Let's give it a try!"

"What will we use to **warm** it?" Nicky asked.

"I know!" Colette squeaked. "I'll get my fur dryer!"

"Be **careful**," Pam reminded her friends. "We can't let the paper touch the fur dryer or it might **burn**, and that could be dangerous."

She blew some warm air onto the paper. Slowly, the CLUE became visible right before their eyes!

CLUE TO FIND THE TIME CAPSULE

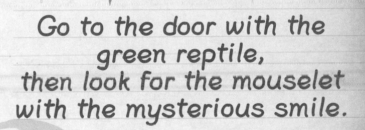

Go to the door with the
green reptile,
then look for the mouselet
with the mysterious smile.

TREASURE HUNT!

"The Gecko Club!" Violet squeaked. "There is a green gecko decoration on the door!"

"You're right!" Nicky cried. "**LET'S GO!**"

They raced through the building and burst into the Gecko Club's clubhouse without even knocking! The rodents looked up from their poetry books, **SURPRISED**.

Huh?

What's up?

"What are you doing here?" Craig asked.

"Sorry for BARGING IN," Paulina apologized. "We are searching for a time capsule, and the first CLUE led us here."

She showed them the secret message in the diary page. "Now we just need to find a mouselet with a **mysterious smile**."

"Well, to be honest, the only mouselet allowed in our club is her," Ryder said, pointing to a PAINTING on the wall. "That portrait was in this room when we started the club."

"That looks like a **mysterious smile** to me!" Colette said.

She took the portrait off the wall and found the SECOND CLUE taped to the back!

Nicky read it out loud. "**DIG** in the **garden** that has no **rose**, but first take a seat where the **rosemary** grows."

"The **HERB GARDEN**!" Shen exclaimed. "There are no roses planted there, but there are a lot of herbs."

They all raced to the herb garden and **SEARCHED** for the rosemary. Paulina spotted it first.

"Here's the rosemary," she said, going to a green, **spiky** plant.

"The rhyme says to <u>take a seat</u> where the rosemary grows," Tanja said. "And look! There's a bench right in front of it."

"The clue said we had to **DIG** in the garden," Pam remembered. "We should dig under the bench!"

"I'll get a **SHOVEL**!" Ron cried. He ran to the garden shed and came back with one. Then they all took turns **digging**.

They dug about a foot deep and didn't find anything. Then . . . **CLANK!** The shovel hit something hard.

Violet **carefully** brushed the dirt aside and removed a faded tin box from the ground. Then she opened it up, revealing its **precious** contents . . .

RUBY WON'T GIVE UP!

The Thea Sisters were happy that they had found the time capsule. But Ruby Flashyfur was in a **terrible** mood.

Her plan to end the poetry club had failed. The mouselets had found a new clubhouse. And everybody on campus was talking about that silly **time capsule**. But what really **upset** Ruby was the scrap of paper that fell out of Alicia's notebook.

"The sky is **BLUE** when I miss **YOU**," Ruby read aloud. She frowned. "Alicia, are you writing poetry?"

"That's **MINE**!" Alicia snatched it back.

Ruby put her paws on her hips. "You're thinking of joining that **silly** club!"

Zoe answered for Alicia. "What's wrong with that? It looks like FUN!"

"I think so, too," Connie chimed in.

"Are you SERIOUS?" Ruby asked, narrowing her eyes at her friends.

"Of course," Connie replied. "And, anyway,

we can get **extra credit** from Professor Rattcliff if we join the club."

Ruby's whiskers twitched. "**Traitors!**" she cried. Then she **crumpled** up the poem, **TOSSED** it behind her, and **STOMPED** toward her dorm room.

There had to be a way to **STOP** the poetry club! And she vowed to find it.

As she passed through the main garden, she heard a familiar voice.

"Vi, don't even **joke** about it!" Colette was saying.

She sounded so **serious** that Ruby stopped to listen. Maybe the conversation could be **useful** to her.

"But I have **no right** to belong to the club," Violet said sadly.

"That's not true," Colette said.

"But it is!" Violet protested. "I'm the only

one who hasn't read a *poem* yet."

"Don't lose **heart**," Nicky told her. "The inspiration will come to you."

Violet decided it was time to tell her friends the truth. She took a deep breath.

"It's not the inspiration I need," she admitted. "It's the COURAGE!"

Colette hugged her. "Oh, Violet! We'll

You can do it, Vi!

help you overcome your **shyness**."

"That's right," Pamela agreed. "The club wouldn't be the same without you. If you **quit**, we all **quit**!"

Ruby sneered as she heard those words. "Really? Would the Thea Sisters give up the club so easily? Then they must not care about it all that much," she said, and a WICKED smile appeared on her face. "I think I know two rodents who would be interested in that **news** . . ."

Heh, heh, heh...

Concerned and Worried

Dear Diary,

The planning of the magazine is going really well. We finally decided to create a poetry magazine with poems by students from Mouseford Academy and the Academy di Mouzza.

We started out with great energy, but now I'm concerned that something's wrong. Elena and Teresa have been avoiding my friends and me, and I'm not sure why. Although I do have a

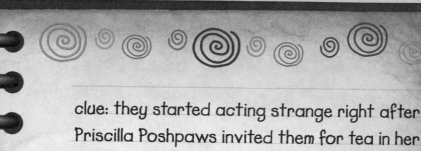

clue: they started acting strange right after Priscilla Poshpaws invited them for tea in her suite. Could Priscilla have something to do with this?

We're all getting together in an hour for a final meeting before our presentation. I hope we can figure things out!

Until later,
M. R. 🙂

RUBY'S RECIPE FOR TROUBLE!

Ruby loved making trouble for the Thea Sisters, and she knew just how to **THREATEN** the poetry club. The conversation she'd just heard had given her an idea.

RECIPE FOR DECEPTION

1 Take some words you overheard . . .

2 Sift in some lies . . .

3 Then sprinkle in a dash of deceit!

BLAH BLAH BLAH BLAH

BLAH BLAH BLAH

BLAH

BLAH BLAH BLAH

With her **PLAN** in place, Ruby went to Elly and Tanja's room right away.

"Hi, Ruby," Tanja said with a smile.

"Can I come in?" Ruby asked, making sure she had a *serious* look on her snout. "There's something I think you should know."

Tanja and Elly looked at her *curiously* as she stepped inside.

"I think your friends are going to start a new poetry club — **without you**!" Ruby began.

Tanja and Elly looked at each other.

"That can't be **true**," Elly said.

"I overheard them talking," Ruby said. "Violet said that she wanted to drop out of the club, and the others said they would follow her."

Tanja frowned. "Well, it's true that Violet

Ha, ha!

A new club?

hasn't read any of her poems yet . . ."

Ruby nodded. "And I know it was your idea, Tanja, for members of the club to read poems out loud. So I'm sure they'll form a **new club** where they can make their **own rules**."

"And you really HEARD them say this?" Elly asked.

"I heard them talking, yes," Ruby replied slyly.

She **quickly** left the room before they could ask any more questions.

That **NiGHT**, when the Thea Sisters got

to their clubhouse for the meeting, Tanja and Elly weren't there.

Colette texted them, and she got this reply:

From: Elly
We're not coming today. You should have told us you didn't want us in the club!

"What is she talking about?" Pam wondered. "That makes no sense."

"This has to be a **misunderstanding**," Nicky said. "Let's go find them and clear this up!"

"I'll just put the diary back until later," Violet said. "Be right there!"

The diary!

Her friends left to find Tanja and Elly, and Violet went to return the diary to the **high** shelf where they had been storing it for safekeeping. She stood on the tips of her paws and reached up, but the book SLIPPED from her paws. It fell down and landed **open**. When Violet picked it up, she started to read the page . . .

Violet finished reading the diary just as her **friends** returned.

THE STRENGTH OF FRIENDSHIP

Dear Diary,

My sixth sense was correct: Elena and Teresa were avoiding us, and it was all because of that interfering Priscilla!

Priscilla is used to getting everything she wants, and I think she realized that she might not win the magazine contest. A lot of the other students have been talking about how much they admire our idea for a poetry magazine. She must have thought we were her biggest competition, so she decided to sabotage us!

How did she do it? She told Elena and Teresa a bunch of lies to try to break up our group!

But we were not about to give up on Elena and Teresa. Charlotte, Sunny, Deb, Pilar, and I wrote them a letter and slid it under the door of their room. It was an invitation to meet us at the Trevi Fountain, along with two coins.

We waited anxiously at the fountain and were so happy to see them show up! Then I held up a coin of my own. There is a legend that if you throw a coin into the fountain over your left shoulder with

your right paw, you will return
to Rome. But I had another
idea.

"I want to make another wish," I said. "That
our friendship with you will be stronger than
any misunderstandings!"

Elena and Teresa smiled, and we started
talking. Priscilla had lied and told them we
didn't want to work on the magazine with
them. But they believed us when we told them
it wasn't true! Then everything went back to
the way it was.

All's well that ends well!
M. R. ☺

Unfortunately, they had **bad news**.

"Elly and Tanja weren't in their room — or they're not answering the door," Nicky reported. "But we ran into Shen. He heard Ruby tell them that we were going to form a poetry club without them, and they **BELIEVED** her!"

Violet looked at the diary and **smiled**. The pages she had just read had given her a great **idea**!

"Don't worry, I know what to do," she said. "The Thea Sisters **never give up**!"

The next morning, Elly and Tanja found a **mysterious** invitation under their door . . .

A MYSTERIOUS INVITATION . . .

"**What's this?**" Elly wondered, picking up the two **notes** from the floor. She handed one to Tanja.

"They're addressed to our *poetry* nicknames," Tanja said.

Curious, the two mouselets went to the clubhouse that night. When they got there,

Dear Liliya,
Please come to this afternoon's poetry club meeting for an important discussion . . .

Dear Sea Star,
Please come to this afternoon's poetry club ...g for an important ...ussion . . .

the room was dim, with only the LIGHT of the electric candles flickering.

"Is anybody here?" Tanja called out.

The Thea Sisters stepped out of the **SHADOWS**. "We're so glad you're here!" Colette said. "Please don't leave."

"We don't know what Ruby told you, but please give us a chance to clear things up," Paulina added.

Nicky grabbed Elly's and Tanya's paws. "There is only one poetry club, and it has **seven** members!" she said. "The club will only survive if we all STICK TOGETHER."

"So you don't want to make up your own CLUB with its own rules?" Tanja asked.

"We never said anything like that," Pam said. "Violet was going to **quit**, and we rallied around her."

"It meant a lot to me," Violet said shyly.

"And so does this club. So I've thought of something we can do to **SYMBOLIZE** our friendship."

She reached into a bag and pulled out a pretty, **GREEN** tin box.

I have an idea!

"These are all the **objects** we brought to our first poetry meeting," she said. "We can take them back now and end the club, if that's what everyone wants to do."

Tanja and Elly were *silent*, thinking.

"Or we can use these to make our own **time capsule**!" Violet finished, and Tanja and Elly both smiled.

"I'm **sorry** we believed Ruby," Elly said.

"That was **foolish** of us," Tanja agreed.

"We will never doubt your **friendship** again, we promise!"

The seven mouselets hugged each other, relieved that the **misunderstanding** was over.

"The time capsule idea is great!" Elly added. "Where should we hide it?"

This box will be our time capsule!

"Why not hide it in the same place that we found the first time capsule?" Colette asked. "That would be a nice TRĬBUTE to those Mouseford students from forty years ago."

"That's a **fabumouse** idea!" Pam cheered, and everyone agreed.

"Do you have your invitations?" Violet asked. "I thought we could each tie a *ribbon* around the box."

Tanja undid the **YELLOW** ribbon from her invite and tied it around the box. Elly did the same with her **BLUE** ribbon.

The Thea Sisters each had a ribbon, too, that matched the **color** of their poetry notebooks. They tied their ribbons around the box, securing it.

"**Perfect**!" said Violet. "Now there's just one thing left to do."

"Bury it?" Pam asked.

Violet grinned. "No. *We should finish reading the diary first!* I am so curious to find out who won the magazine contest."

Her friends agreed, and they sat down on the big floor pillows, eager to hear the end of the story . . .

I Am So Shy . . .

Dear Diary,

There are only a few days left until the end of the summer session, and Charlotte, Deb, Pilar, Sunny, and I have been making the most of them!

Today we went to visit the enormouse Vatican Museum, and then had lunch in the very lively Trastevere neighborhood. We ate an amazing

**Via dei Colli
Roma**

CREMOSA

*The best cheese
pie in Rome*

cheese pie, and the friendly owner of the restaurant gave me the recipe. I can't wait to try it!

We have not forgotten about our assignment. We added the finishing touches and our magazine is now ready to present – and my friends want me to do it!

The thing is — I don't know if I can. I'm worried that my shyness will take over. Can you imagine? I would have to speak in front of hundreds of students! I am sure my paws will shake, and I won't be able to utter a single word.

What should I do? I'm so confused. Maybe I should go for a walk.

Until later,
M. R. ☺

TiME TO
iNVESTiGATE!

"PLEASE, PLEASE, PLEASE keep reading!"
Colette pleaded.

"We have to find out what M. R. decided,"
Pam urged.

"YESSSSS!" the others squeaked.

Violet turned the page and gasped. "The
rest of the pages are BLANK! The diary
ends here!" she announced.

The mouselets LOOKED at each other
in shock.

"Does this mean that we will never know
how the summer ended for our friends
from the past?" Elly asked.

Everyone thought for a moment.
Paulina piped up first.

"I have an id·ea! We can look for M. R., Pilar, Charlotte, Deb, and Sunny and invite them to Mouseford for a reunion," she said. "They can tell us the ending themselves!"

"That would be mouserific, but how will we find them?" Colette asked.

"We can LOOK through school records," Nicky suggested.

"And the Internet should be helpful, too," Tanja said.

Let's look here . . .

"This will be a big **INVESTIGATION**," Paulina said. "I think we might need more mice."

They asked the Gecko Club to help, and the rodents agreed. They divided into **TEAMS**. Elly, Nicky, and Violet looked through the old records. Paulina, Tanja, and Shen searched the **Internet**.

Pam, Colette, Craig, and Ron decided to ask rodents around the **iSLAND** if they

Nothing yet . . .

remembered the five mouselets.

"Let's start at the **CHEESE HOUSE DINER**," Pam said. "A lot of the island old-timers hang out there, and besides, I could go for a snack."

MITCH MELTER, the owner of the diner, welcomed them with a big smile. "Hello there," he said. "Did the wind carry the appetizing aroma of **cheese fondue** all the way to Mouseford?"

Welcome!

Colette sniffed the air. "We'll definitely order some," she said. "But first, we have a question. We're trying to **TRACK DOWN** some students who went to Mouseford Academy forty years ago."

"Forty years ago?" Mitch

asked. "That's before my **TIME**, but talk to Oscar over there. He's got a great memory."

He pointed to an elderly FISHERMOUSE reading a newspaper. The four students approached him and introduced themselves. Colette told him their story.

That's Oscar!

"Charlotte, Sunny, Pilar, and Deb?" Oscar repeated. "Hmm. The name Sunny rings a **bell**. I remember a Sunny who was a great **SAILBOAT** racer."

"That could be her!" Pam said. "The Sunny we read about is very **ATHLETIC**."

Oscar stood up. "Let's check the bulletin board. There are lots of **PHOTOS** of the old **RACING** championships."

They examined the photos, and sure enough, there was a photo of a mouselet

named **Sunny**, holding a trophy!

"That photo is dated the same year as the *diary*!" Colette said, her voice filled with excitement.

"And her **FiRST**

and **last** name is on the back, so we can contact her," Pam said.

Ron gave Oscar a hug. "**Thanks!** You really helped us!"

Just then the **door** to the diner OPENED, and their friends poured in.

"We just found Sunny's last name!" Pam exclaimed when she saw them.

"And we **found** Charlotte's and Deb's last names!" Nicky **squeaked**.

Tanja held out a piece of PAPER. "We even got Pilar's address!"

"But we still have no CLUE who M.R. is," Violet announced sadly.

The mouselets were all quiet for a moment, until Colette piped up.

"Let's not get discouraged," she said. "We can ask Charlotte, Sunny, Deb, and Pilar to invite their mysterious friend to the reunion for us."

"That's perfect!" Violet cried. "What are we waiting for? Let's send those *invitations*."

LET THE REUNION BEGIN!

The students quickly mailed out the invitations. Charlotte, Pilar, Deb, and Sunny replied right away, and they all seemed to be just as excited and **cheerful** as the mouselets described in the diary!

The poetry club members got to work **PLANNING** the reunion. When the day came, they were ready to welcome the **GUESTS OF HONOR**. Pam went to the dock to pick them up, while the others patiently waited . . . and waited . . . and waited . . .

When the car appeared, they saw that Pam wasn't driving. An older mouselet with **WAVY** brown hair was at the wheel. She

was the **FiRSt** out of the car.

"We're finally here!" she said. "**Back at our beloved Mouseford!**"

"Sorry we're **late**," Pam apologized as she helped the other three guests out of the backseat of the car. "Deb insisted on driving."

Welcome back to Mouseford!

"And of course she had to do it on the **bumpiest** road on the whole island!" said a blonde rodent dressed in **PINK**. The mouselets quickly guessed that she must be Charlotte.

You must be the Thea Sisters!

Charlotte's friends burst out laughing.

"It's like no *time* has passed at all," remarked Pilar, a mouse with a chic blonde haircut.

"It's so good to see everyone again!" agreed Sunny, a gray rodent wearing a RED SCARF.

The Thea Sisters approached them. "Welcome to Mouseford!" Violet squeaked.

"We're so HAPPY you're here, but we're SORRY M.R. didn't come," Colette said sadly.

"What do you mean?" Pilar asked, confused. "She told me she would be here."

"And here I am!" a familiar voice exclaimed.

Everyone turned to see Professor Rattcliff standing there.

"Margaret!" Charlotte, Deb, Pilar, and Sunny shouted all at once. Then they ran to **hug** their friend.

The members of the Poets' Club looked at one another, surprised. M.R., the mysterious writer of the diary, was Professor Margaret Rattcliff!

Here I am!

A HAPPY REUNION

Once they got over their surprise, the mouselets decided to invite Charlotte, Deb, Pilar, Sunny, and Margaret to a **special** meeting of the poetry club.

"You've really made this very **cozy**," Professor Rattcliff remarked.

"Thank you for letting us use this room," Colette said, and then she handed her a WRAPPED PACKAGE. "This is for you."

When Margaret opened it, she **gasped**.

"But this is . . . our time capsule!" she squeaked.

"Our time capsule?" Sunny repeated, startled.

"Yes," Elly replied, smiling. "We found it, thanks to the CLUES written in the mysterious diary. Now it's *time* for us to give it back."

The former students gathered around the box and looked through their MEMENTOS.

"Here's the WRENCH I used to fix my car!" Deb exclaimed.

Our mementos!

"I used this MAP so I wouldn't get lost in the school hallways," Pilar remembered, laughing.

Charlotte smiled. "This is the BARRETTE I wore on my first day at Mouseford."

"And these were the *lucky laces* for my running shoes!" Sunny added.

Margaret picked up the

Squeakspeare book. "This book made me fall in **love** with poetry," she said with a sigh.

Then Nicky asked the **QUESTION** they had all been wanting to ask.

"Excuse me, Professor, but we are so **CURIOUS** to know how your summer in Rome ended," Nicky said. "Did you present your group's project?"

"Yes I did," she replied. "Thanks to the SUPPORt of my friends, I was able to overcome my **shyness**. Our magazine won FÏRST PRÏZE!"

"Why didn't you write that in your diary?" Violet asked.

The professor looked at her and smiled. "I realized that because of my shyness, I was only writing about an **ADVENTURE** instead of *living* it!"

Violet understood. At the meetings of the poetry club, she had been a **SPECTATOR**, staying on the <u>sidelines</u> because she was afraid she wasn't good enough. But right then she realized something: if young Margaret Rattcliff could OVERCOME her shyness, she could, too!

Violet took a deep breath and faced her friends. She could see the **love** and

SUPPORT in their faces, and that gave her courage.

"I WOULD LOVE . . . TO READ YOU ONE OF MY POEMS!" Violet announced.

Everyone clapped encouragingly. Violet took a **deep breath** and began to read.

It was a poem about **friendship**, of course, because Violet had always known: with her friends behind her, she could do anything!

Don't miss any of these exciting *Thea Sisters* adventures!

Thea Stilton and the Dragon's Code

Thea Stilton and the Mountain of Fire

Thea Stilton and the Ghost of the Shipwreck

Thea Stilton and the Secret City

Thea Stilton and the Mystery in Paris

Thea Stilton and the Cherry Blossom Adventure

Thea Stilton and the Star Castaways

Thea Stilton: Big Trouble in the Big Apple

Thea Stilton and the Ice Treasure

Thea Stilton and the Secret of the Old Castle

Thea Stilton and the Blue Scarab Hunt

Thea Stilton and the Prince's Emerald

Thea Stilton and the Mystery on the Orient Express

Thea Stilton and the Dancing Shadows

Thea Stilton and the Legend of the Fire Flowers

Thea Stilton and the Spanish Dance Mission

Thea Stilton and the Journey to the Lion's Den

Thea Stilton and the Great Tulip Heist

Thea Stilton and the Chocolate Sabotage

Thea Stilton and the Missing Myth

Thea Stilton and the Lost Letters

Thea Stilton and the Tropical Treasure

Thea Stilton and the Hollywood Hoax

Thea Stilton and the Madagascar Madness

Don't miss any of these Mouseford Academy adventures!

#1 Drama at Mouseford #2 The Missing Diary #3 Mouselets in Danger #4 Dance Challenge #5 The Secret Invention

#6 A Mouseford Musical #7 Mice Take the Stage #8 A Fashionable Mystery #9 The Mysterious Love Letter #10 A Dream on Ice

#11 Lights, Camera, Action! #12 Mice on the Runway #13 Sea Turtle Rescue #14 The Secret Notebook

Be sure to read all my fabumouse adventures!

#1 Lost Treasure of the Emerald Eye

#2 The Curse of the Cheese Pyramid

#3 Cat and Mouse in a Haunted House

#4 I'm Too Fond of My Fur!

#5 Four Mice Deep in the Jungle

#6 Paws Off, Cheddarface!

#7 Red Pizzas for a Blue Count

#8 Attack of the Bandit Cats

#9 A Fabumouse Vacation for Geronimo

#10 All Because of a Cup of Coffee

#11 It's Halloween, You 'Fraidy Mouse!

#12 Merry Christmas, Geronimo!

#13 The Phantom of the Subway

#14 The Temple of the Ruby of Fire

#15 The Mona Mousa Code

#16 A Cheese-Colored Camper

#17 Watch Your Whiskers, Stilton!

#18 Shipwreck on the Pirate Islands

#19 My Name Is Stilton, Geronimo Stilton

#20 Surf's Up, Geronimo!

#21 The Wild, Wild West

#22 The Secret of Cacklefur Castle

A Christmas Tale

#23 Valentine's Day Disaster

#24 Field Trip to Niagara Falls

#25 The Search for Sunken Treasure

#26 The Mummy with No Name

#27 The Christmas Toy Factory

#28 Wedding Crasher

#29 Down and Out Down Under

#30 The Mouse Island Marathon

#31 The Mysterious Cheese Thief

Christmas Catastrophe

#32 Valley of the Giant Skeletons

#33 Geronimo and the Gold Medal Mystery

#34 Geronimo Stilton, Secret Agent

#35 A Very Merry Christmas

#36 Geronimo's Valentine

#37 The Race Across America

#38 A Fabumouse School Adventure

#39 Singing Sensation

#40 The Karate Mouse

#41 Mighty Mount Kilimanjaro

#42 The Peculiar Pumpkin Thief

#43 I'm Not a Supermouse!

#44 The Giant Diamond Robbery

#45 Save the White Whale!

#46 The Haunted Castle

#47 Run for the Hills, Geronimo!

#48 The Mystery in Venice

#49 The Way of the Samurai

#50 This Hotel Is Haunted!

#51 The Enormouse Pearl Heist

#52 Mouse in Space!

#53 Rumble in the Jungle

#54 Get into Gear, Stilton!

#55 The Golden Statue Plot

#56 Flight of the Red Bandit

The Hunt for the Golden Book

#57 The Stinky Cheese Vacation

#58 The Super Chef Contest

#59 Welcome to Moldy Manor

The Hunt for the Curious Cheese

#60 The Treasure of Easter Island

#61 Mouse House Hunter

#62 Mouse Overboard!

The Hunt for the Secret Papyrus

#63 The Cheese Experiment

#64 Magical Mission

#65 Bollywood Burglary

The Hunt for the Hundredth Key

#66 Operation: Secret Recipe

Be sure to read all of our magical special edition adventures!

THE KINGDOM OF FANTASY

THE QUEST FOR PARADISE:
THE RETURN TO THE KINGDOM OF FANTASY

THE AMAZING VOYAGE:
THE THIRD ADVENTURE IN THE KINGDOM OF FANTASY

THE DRAGON PROPHECY:
THE FOURTH ADVENTURE IN THE KINGDOM OF FANTASY

THE VOLCANO OF FIRE:
THE FIFTH ADVENTURE IN THE KINGDOM OF FANTASY

THE SEARCH FOR TREASURE:
THE SIXTH ADVENTURE IN THE KINGDOM OF FANTASY

THE ENCHANTED CHARMS:
THE SEVENTH ADVENTURE IN THE KINGDOM OF FANTASY

THE PHOENIX OF DESTINY:
AN EPIC KINGDOM OF FANTASY ADVENTURE

THE HOUR OF MAGIC:
THE EIGHTH ADVENTURE IN THE KINGDOM OF FANTASY

THE WIZARD'S WAND:
THE NINTH ADVENTURE IN THE KINGDOM OF FANTASY

THEA STILTON: THE JOURNEY TO ATLANTIS

THEA STILTON: THE SECRET OF THE FAIRIES

THEA STILTON: THE SECRET OF THE SNOW

THEA STILTON: THE CLOUD CASTLE

THEA STILTON: THE TREASURE OF THE SEA

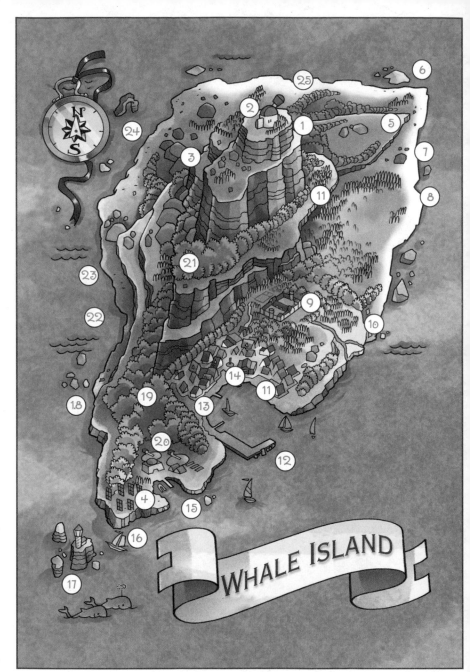

WHALE ISLAND

MAP OF WHALE ISLAND

THANKS FOR READING, AND GOOD-BYE UNTIL OUR NEXT ADVENTURE!

Thea Sisters